This book belongs to:

_____

Belle

Cogsworth

The Beast

Lumiere

Mrs Potts
& Chip

STARRING

This edition published
by Parragon in 2007
Parragon
Queen Street House
4 Queen Street
Bath, BA1 1HE, UK

ISBN 978-1-4054-8013-0
Printed in China

DISNEY's
Beauty and the Beast

Bath · New York · Singapore · Hong Kong · Cologne · Delhi · Melbourne

Once upon a time, a
selfish young prince refused to
give an old beggar-woman shelter in
his castle. But the old woman was really
an enchantress. As punishment, she turned
the prince into a terrifying beast and cast a
spell on everyone in the castle.
Giving the Beast a magic rose she said,
"This will bloom until your twenty-first year.
If you learn to love another and earn that
person's love before the last petal falls,
the spell will be broken. If not,
you will remain a Beast
forever."

In a sleepy
village nearby, an
eccentric inventor
named Maurice lived
with his beautiful
daughter Belle.
Gaston, a strong
and handsome young man
from the village, had decided
that he wanted to make Belle his wife.

"After all," he told his friend Lefou,
"she's the best-looking girl
in town. And I deserve
the best!"

Gaston arrived
at Belle's house,
confident that
Belle would agree
to marry him. But, when he
asked her, Belle refused him without a second thought.
She knew she could never marry someone as arrogant
and conceited as Gaston!

One day Maurice set off for a fair with his latest invention. As night fell he lost his way and had to seek refuge in the Beast's castle.

Maurice was welcomed by some friendly, enchanted servants, including a candelabra named Lumiere, a clock named Cogsworth, a teapot named Mrs Potts and her son Chip, a teacup.

But the Beast was furious when he discovered a stranger in his home and he threw Maurice into the dungeon. When Maurice's horse returned home alone, Belle set off at once to search for her father.

"Oh, Papa," Belle cried when she found Maurice in the freezing dungeon, "we must get you out of here!"

Sensing danger, Belle
turned round. There was the
Beast, towering over her and
growling loudly.

"Please let my father go,"
Belle pleaded. "I'll take his place here."

The Beast agreed at once. He dragged Maurice out
of the cell and sent him back to the village.

The Beast showed
Belle to her room.
"You can go
anywhere in the
castle," he told her,
"except the West
Wing. That is forbidden!"

Poor Belle was miserable!
She missed her father and her home. The enchanted
objects prepared a wonderful meal for her and tried to
cheer her up with their
singing and dancing.

But Belle was still lonely and later that night she wandered through the castle. She soon found herself in the West Wing. There, among broken furniture and cracked mirrors, she found the magic rose, its petals drooping sadly.

Just as Belle reached out to touch the rose, the Beast burst in howling with rage. Terrified, Belle ran out into the snowy night.

Belle leapt on
to her father's horse
and set off blindly into
the dark forest.

Suddenly, she was
surrounded by a pack of vicious, hungry wolves. Just as the
wolves closed in for the kill, the Beast appeared through
the trees. Fighting bravely, he drove the wolves away.

But then the Beast sank to the ground in pain. The wolves had injured him! Belle knew she could not leave him there alone.

She took the Beast back to the castle and gently tended his bleeding wounds.

He seemed quite different now and she was no longer frightened of him.

Meanwhile, at the village tavern, Gaston was still brooding over Belle, even though his friends did their best to cheer him up. Suddenly, the door burst open and Maurice raced in.

"Help!" he cried. "Belle is being held prisoner by a monstrous Beast!"

The men in the tavern burst out laughing. They thought Maurice was mad! But Gaston smiled to himself. He had thought of a way to make Belle marry him! He called a tall, sinister-looking man over to his table and Gaston began to tell him what he had in mind.

As the days passed, Belle and the Beast spent more and more time together. The enchanted servants were delighted. They were certain that Belle would fall in love with their master and break the spell. But time was running out. Each day more petals fell from the magic rose.

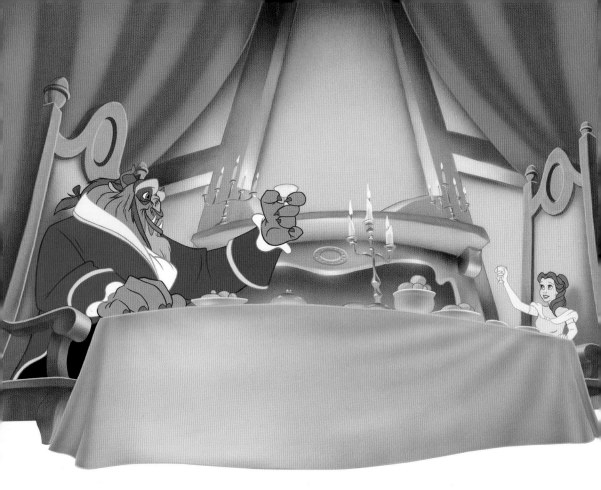

One evening, after dining and dancing
together, the Beast and Belle sat out on
the terrace in the cool night air.

"Are you happy here, Belle?"
asked the Beast.

"Yes," replied
Belle. "I just wish
I could see my
father again."

"You can," said the Beast, and he gave Belle a magic mirror. "This will show you whatever you wish."

"Oh, thank you!" exclaimed Belle. But, as she gazed into it, Belle saw her father lost and trembling with cold as he searched for Belle!

Although the Beast loved Belle, he knew he had to let her go to her father. "Take the mirror with you," he said sadly, "so you can remember me."

Belle set off from the castle and soon found Maurice. She brought him safely home and put him to bed.

The next day Gaston arrived at Belle's house with a crowd of villagers. He said that Maurice would be taken to an asylum unless Belle agreed to marry him.

"My father's not mad!" cried Belle.

"He must be," said Lefou. "He was raving about a monstrous beast!"

"The Beast
is real!" cried
Belle. "Look!"
She held up the
magic mirror and
the crowd saw the
Beast for themselves.
They all shouted with fear
and refused to listen to Belle when she told them the
Beast was kind and good.

Furious that his plan had failed, Gaston gathered
the mob together to attack the Beast's castle.

The men
marched up to
the castle doors
and broke them
down. Cogsworth
led the enchanted
servants in a brave
defence of the castle.
But the Beast missed Belle
and was too heartbroken to fight, even when Gaston beat
him with a club and drove him
on to the castle roof.

Only when he heard
Belle's voice did the
Beast look up.

"You came back!"
he cried, rushing to
embrace Belle.

This was the
chance Gaston had
been waiting for.

Drawing his dagger,
he stabbed the Beast
in the back. But as
the Beast collapsed,
Gaston tripped – and
fell tumbling from
the roof.

Belle ran to the wounded Beast and bent to kiss him. The last petal was just about to fall from the rose.

"You can't die," sobbed Belle. "I love you! I wish I had never left you alone!"

Suddenly, a magic mist surrounded the Beast and, before Belle's astonished eyes, he changed into the handsome young prince he had once been.

One by one, the enchanted servants became human again. Weeping with joy, they hugged each other as the Prince swept Belle into his arms.

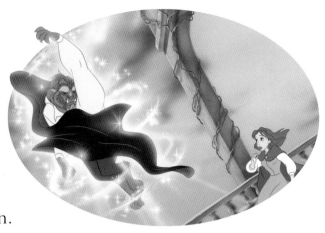

The Prince had found his true love at last and the spell of the enchantress was broken. As the sun burst through the clouds, they knew they would all live together in happiness for ever after.